Hell's Press Presents

First paperback edition 2023

ISBN   978-1-7381321-1-9   (paperback)
ISBN   978-1-7381322-0-1   (ebook)

hellspress.com

Fairie Tales

Red Riding Hood and Bo Peep

COUNT FATHOM

Dedicated to...

...you, the enslaved, though you know it not. Protected, you think you are. A Charter, you say you have. Rights this paper gives you. Perversion do I say. An echo of a sentiment forgotten in the fray.

The right you have to freedom is not given, but taken away. Freedom is a birthright to every living thing, from the smallest, meekest warbler to the mighty sceptred king.

If each, in his own right, entered into a contract with each other to produce a government, then would fate applaud.

The rights I've been given are a meagre few. Applauded occasionally for their brevity no less. Boil and bubble, toil and trouble, a poison in the air I confess. Those who would enslave me and would force me to behave, will not rob me of my right to profess.

What you hear ahead will step on morals. Stomp not tread. I want no quarrels, just imagination spread.

Inspired by Thomas Paine

Table of Contents

Preface

You've been through one already and now you're back for more. But that was just a taste, a morsel, ornament, décor. You're wondering now if that's the end, what else I have in store.

You've met our Jack, his giant love, and you thought good and right. If love is true, it overcomes the difference in their height. It's time to send a shot your way and give you quite a fright.

I'm not the man you think I am, we've only just begun. I'll not allow you think me well, ideals must be undone. I'm loud and brash and full of scorn, I'll burn you like the sun.

Here comes spite and hatefulness in stories two and three. Not from me, but from the hoard, who won't forgive a barren moral tree. I disdain their righteous sense of staunch morality.

My Heroines are beautiful, but victims they are not. Nor are they models for the children, chaste and pure, that stuff is rot. They are people, they are animals, their lives are tied in knots.

These women are not helpless, they just do the best they can. They look out for themselves, they plot, they scheme, they form a plan. And yes, it's true, their path to fortune sometimes leads them to a man.

Heroines they are to me, for them I have respect. Herein a moral looseness is not counted a defect. Self-reliance is the measure, for their very lives they must protect.

Anyway you'll hate me, that I'm sure of, that I know. You'll hate until you shiver, til you're hot enough to glow. Enough foreplay now, you're ready for it, let's begin the show.

Bo Peep

"Bethany Ann Olivia John." Those were the last words of Marshal Peep, coal miner by trade and dead at 26. They were to be the names of his only child, a girl, one last final insult from god, as he saw things, before his soul detached forever from his mortal shell.

She was a precocious child, forever asking why of whomever was nearest. She certainly didn't intend to annoy people, and nor did she, at least the men. An adorable child, treated kindly and thinking all received the same. In adolescence she was aware, as men would clutch their hearts and sigh at the sight of her. By maturity Betsy Peep, whom everyone called Bo, was at the height of her influence, and she knew it too. It had been years already since she had paid for anything. Shopkeeps would fill a bag for her and scurry her off before the wife returned, invariably justifying their charity for not so little Bo with a flippant "Her father's dead and her mother's a drunk whore with one foot in the grave."

Which was true. Her mother put the other foot in just then, leaving Bo orphaned at the end of her formative years, but not without some sage parting advice with which Bo could secure her position in life, "You're dumb as a toad, Bo. Marry rich or you'll starve once your looks go." Bo, not

such a fool as to think herself a genius, was
still a little hurt by this final presumption of
her mother. But she took the advice to heart,
like a sensible girl would, and this story will
tell you how she went about it.

Though she would follow the advice
of her dying mother and behave as a sensible
girl would, Bo was, in fact, not sensible at
all, and had quite a time of it in the begin-
ning of her quest. That very day she pushed
herself up against Peter Peppers, thinking
him a fitting candidate, and Peter responded
quite favourably, renting out local accom-
modations for the evening, where they could
talk it over. Bo willingly and enthusiastically
shed the petals of her flower that night, and
slept wonderfully. Peter went home to his
family before the sun set, and Bo etched the

first of her commandments – no married men.

Well.. at least the married one's wouldn't do as true candidates. But a little practice couldn't hurt, and Bo was pleased with this compromise. As you can imagine, it wasn't long before Bo found herself unwelcome over much of the town.

"What a frustrating position I'm in!" thought poor Bo, and then laughed when she remembered the position she'd been in earlier that day.

Bo plopped down in the long grass, picked petals off petunias, and puzzled out a plan. She'd have to move. Maybe more than once. Her mother had always said 'second best is first worst', and Bo resolved to reach high.

With this in mind, Bo mobilized
for a move to the metropolis. All the family belongings were sold, as was their fine
little cottage on the outskirts of the village.
Money wouldn't be a problem for some
time, and the relief and security afforded by
funds of this sort allow people to reach for
their dreams.

The city was some ways off, and Bo
would spend four days in and out of stop
over rooms along the way, not once spending the night alone. A butcher, a baker, a
candlestick maker, and on the third night
she had all three. Rub-a-dub-dub, there was
room in the tub, for whom do you think
it be? Three lucky men, to find such a hen,
that gave it all out for free. They pooled
together and left some money on the dresser

before going their separate ways, down what tangled paths we are never to hear of again.

Bo considered the money. This was new. She had been given gifts before, but this was the first time she had received money for sex. Bo contemplated the prospects of the two paths before her. If she began accepting money, Bo was sure she could amass a small fortune over a decade and live off the proceeds, independent to the grave. But in her soul Bo did not want to take money for sex. She loved sex! And taking money means you are performing a service, so you'd better perform it well if you want to be successful. She would be competing for those dollars in the trade, and that would sap the joy from her sexuality, a part of herself she loved. Finally, advertising herself as a hooker would forever bar her from changing course and choosing the other path, lest she was willing to start all over again in another town.

A wise woman was her mother, and Betsy would commit to the plan recommended for a girl of her ability and charm. She would daily be depleting her principle funds, but only until such time as she could accomplish an advantageous marriage.

A pure reputation was necessary to bait her fish, so hooking was not acceptable. First, she needed access to the lake where her fish lived.

Bo scouted the richest areas in town over several nights, and charted a course with some good chance of success. Each night a house on any given street lit up like a child given cake, and people would come and go in fine clothes. Bo took note of the women's dress, and had tailored for herself something suitably chaste, yet with the promise of sin. She liked a dress loose below the waist, so she could whet the appetite.

Bo marched confidently, behind a couple, straight up the walkway to a mansion soiree on just one such night.

The butler's head inclined attentively. "I'm Bethany Ann Olivia John. I've been invited by the deputy vice consul for district court 13. I've come with news. Here, take my coat please, thank you. Don't bother, I'll find him myself." A good plan might take some nerve, and Ms. Peep was in no short supply, with the audacity of an airborne aardvark.

First impressions were overwhelming for little Bo Peep. There were men and women everywhere, all of whom seemed easy in their clothes amongst the splendour of wealth. Assaulted on all sides by unimaginable luxuries, try as she might, Bo could not maintain a sophisticated urbane disguise. For five whole minutes Bo wandered like a village booby, in and out of rooms unblinking, her jaw hanging loose, wagging to and fro.

But she soon settled into character, stalking likely prey, and there was none likelier than Phillip von Braun von Winken III, heir to the Winken Blinken spectacles fortune. He was a bit on the young side, but swimming in wealth. Sadly, his parents threw her out that very night. It was a culture shock for little Peep, as fourteen was good and right to marry in her village.

Encouraged by the early success of her new method, Bo boldly barged into

yet another evening event, and hooked
William Wellersby Woodcock. Billy Bean,
Antonio Carlos Alejendras, and Francoise
Le France followed. She could hook the fish
well enough. The boys were all too eager,
one proclaiming love, another marriage, and
a third three French hens, among sundry
other goods. Reeling one in proved a pickle
of pronounced proportions.

It would always go wrong for poor
Bo Peep. The first kicked her out on the ride
home for expectorating on the floor, appar-
ently another cultural miscue. She thought
she was being coy and flirtatious when she
flashed the next her panties from the sofa
in the living room. He didn't think so, and
politely hailed her a ride home, red as a
beet. And then she couldn't speak spanish or
french, so those relationships never moved

in the intended direction. All sorts of wrong
directions she had become accustomed to in
a previous life were tried.

Poor Bo! But never lose heart! All was
not lost. She had learned a valuable lesson.
City life was perhaps not best suited to our
heroine after all. She might be a Duchess,
and yet much disgusted. The life of luxury
was a burden to blessed Bo Peep, an upkeep
she'd rather not have. She has grown wiser
before our very eyes. Bo packed up for a
tour of the surrounding countryside, with
a new and delightful plan in mind, well on
her way to fulfilling the wonders of destiny.

Much to your surprise, yet more
petunias were having their petals plucked
just around this time. And just whom do
you think was plucking the petals off those
petunias? This prey is nervous and must me

approached delicately, the story teller moving like a cautious doe. We can't charge right at him, we'll frighten him off. He's skittish. Think how horrible, right at this moment, it would be for him to be discovered picking petunias. We chanced upon a glimpse into the very soul of our unsuspecting hero.

Once, one needed his wits in a heartless, competitive world. Survival of the fittest was nature's sharpest tool. But human technological progress has dulled the blade, and now good and all bear children. Those born into wealth need not compete, living atop an ever growing pile of fiat currency. Their good fortune leads to excellent education, and contacts in industries of every sort, well up and away from some hill of financial security that the sweat stained masses scramble to ascend, slipping, inevitably, at the sheerest cliffs.

Some work hard and, while maybe not quite deserve their good fortune, do earn a good portion of it through their own application. Their successes should be congratulated, but should not be attributed to superior ability. Mankind's treasures are buried under a fleshy mass of poverty, undiscovered and forgotten. Work as they might, the outcome is uncertain for the poor. Caution is a mark of intelligence, further hampering the realization of their potential.

Atop the world, gifting out privilege to the already advantaged few, sit the kings on their thrones of gold, and always a place at the table for kith and kin. Such it has been, and such it will always be. Such it was for Robyn Publick, heir to a vast family estate that stretched over vale and valley, gorge and glen, and bog and basin, so vast that a crow might fall out of the sky before he made the length of it.

Robyn, at present picking petunias to present them as a package to his first cousin Princess Penelope Publick, was raised very gently from his crib and placed into a nominal administrative position in government as a favour to the Publick Trust for making vast returns for the state, in some fishy Public-Publick partnership. This gave Robyn ample time to romance among the clouds on one meadow or another about the estate.

Over the crest of the gently rolling hills swaddling the meadow, descended a heavenly figure lifted from a fairie tale, in a light blue frock trimmed with white frilled blouse, bouncing deliciously down the flowers. Robyn was delighted.

"Pardon me sir, but my sheep have wandered off, and I'm in a fix to find them." How she bent and pressed her knees together! "Have I trespassed on your estate? I'm so very sorry for what I've done. I'm completely at your mercy. Only my sheep! Have you seen them?" At this Bo feigned feint, and went to her hands and knees, crawling needy to poor helpless useless Robyn.

"Just lie here a minute, Miss, and calm yourself. You're in such a blush, I can't hear what you're saying." A welcome invitation and Bo cuddled up close, then pushed her face into his thighs. Some say the prophecy was fulfilled that very moment.

"Maybe you should come back with me, Miss, to the Manor House. We can get cleaned up and refreshed before we have a chat about your wool." And they were off, over the valley and across the vale, through the gorge and past the glen, around the bog, and into the basin, where the Manor House sat, whispering wishes conspiratorially along the way.

This marvel of milkmaid handicraft, so slight and light as to flutter on wings, but with the healthy milk capacity of a ravenous dairy cow, so completely enchanted our impressionable Robyn that vows were exchanged on that very walk. "Mother!", he would say, "Mother will adore you. You're her picture of perfection. Mine too! I'll lather you in luxury and affection." Robyn soon spied his mother, inspecting the gardener's work on the hydrangeas, on the left middle of the back beds.

"Is that you Robyn? Who is that you have with you there? Heaven has opened and dropped us an angel."

There was a sudden warmth to the air, a slowing down in time, the setting of concrete around a legacy.

"Little Bo Peep has lost her sheep and doesn't know where to find them!"

"Leave them alone, and they'll come home, wagging their tales behind them."

Robyn, his mother, and Betsy Ann Olivia John Peep withdrew into the converging mysteries of time, space, and vast fortune.

The End

Red Riding Hood

Sally was a sassy little minx. She would swish left and swish right as she pierced through a crowd in her trademark red riding hood, intent but graceful. Little Red travelled like light among the market people, unimpeded and unimpeding, but always pleasing. She bargained for her purchases with cunning and deceit. The shopkeep rarely minded. The shopkeep's wife, on the other hand, would chase off Sally with a broom when appropriate. That was every

time Red showed up, according to the shopkeep's wife. Red knew all this, and licked her
lips as she watched another wife abandon
her helpless husband at the stall.

Grandma had taught Sally everything
she knew. Grandma was an ace. Grandma
made a fortune on the streets in her day.
Now she was finely ensconced in the family cottage, out the way a bit. A fine little
cottage, surrounded by a fine little fence.
Not a picket fence, for she had taste and that
would be cliché. Trunks of little trees. Not
quite saplings, for that's forbidden. But little
more than, with more money than sense. At
least the one's she was after. Was I talking
about the trees she used for her fence? Right.
Good wood. She polished the bark off,
sanded them down, and stained them. They

made a fine little fence for Grandma around her fine little cottage.

A finely kept carpet of grass decorated her yard. Maybe she'd let it go a little bit, but that happens at her age. And who was she keeping it up for anyhow? That's the way she thought of it. She kept the drapes clean, and those looked great. They still got looks to this day from the admittedly rare passers by. Grandma clearly wasn't quite done with her own sassiness, and could she ever be, really? Some things are innate.

Sally came of an age and Grandma passed on all that she was to Sally, including her lucky red riding hood. Grandma's own mother had worn that riding hood in her time, and Grandma owed much to the cumulative knowledge of family tradition.

Sally respected her matrilineal lineage. She cherished her red riding hood, well willing to take up the mantle with all the feistiness and confidence of youth, but often felt imposed upon to live up to a reputation that she didn't yet deserve. The burden of the hood weighed heavy on her heart, but she felt greatness in her soul.

Sally still went to school, on the advice of Grandma. It was a superb social training ground. After working her way through the student hierarchy, all positions, she was finally expelled for supposedly seducing several of the staff, according to their wives. For the time being, Sally slept at Grandma's during the day.

What about her parents you ask? Who knows about her father, she never had one as far as she knew. Her mother sadly passed of a suspicious syphilitic infection gone wrong, septicemia I think. Sally was only seven. Grandma Sybil, on her mother's side, supported Sally since then.

We might as well get introduced to some of the other characters at this point. Will the axe man steps forward. He supplies Grandma with firewood, no charge. Will can be seen at Grandma's cottage from time to time. He's a big, burly teddy bear. Bears look like that, but they have a temper. Like a lot of wild animals, they commit to an encounter absolutely, their attention never waivers. If he's mad, you can bet he means it. Forewarned is forearmed.

And, of course, the new comer to the glens and dales and forests and woods that cover the ravines and valleys and vales and such about and around Grandma's snug little cottage must be met. The light glints off the silver, streaking through his slightly dishevelled but otherwise almost regal mane of thick warm fur. His steps are measured, he is alert, he is a philosopher of sorts. And he has not met his match, or he wouldn't be alive. He is, of course, the wolf.

Wolf had a lot of territory to cover, but he knew every inch of it. And he was the unquestioned, unchallenged monarch of his realm. An aficionado of fine venison, Wolf stalked his elusive prey across great distances and at great expense. He genuinely enjoyed the hunt. But, like many a monarch before, Wolfie's appetite then extended to the abnormal.

Having satiated his every desire, Wolf had somewhat dulled his lust for life. Being a highly intelligent mammal, he considered his prospects carefully. Wolf was fifty seven wolf years old. How many good years did he have left? Any day now some cub, young and hungry, fresh off of privation, lean and taut, could come and dethrone our hero. Wolf wasn't about to let his life pass him by, resting on his laurels. Meanwhile, he understood that the fate of all wolves was sealed and he would be no exception. Something of the carpe diem seized Wolfie, and he began to look about through new eyes.

Wolfie began to frequent the corner of the woods with the long path, worn over decades of slight though reliable use, that finished at the fine little cottage, so nicely kept in his opinion. He didn't need or want the grass completely mown. He liked it this way. He took a liking to Grandma. So when Wolfie was full he would find his way over to Grandma. It wouldn't do to spend more than a few days a month skulking around about the cottage, for many reasons. While he might be full now, he wouldn't be so in a short while. Best keep track of his prey. The cottage did attract some of the choicest doe, and Wolfie liked that. That was a plus. But humans weren't entirely accepting of wolves, and there was a threat, as many of them were about these parts of the woods. He'd seen that axe man more than once. That axe man was no joke. Wolfie had given him a snarl of warning, and out came that axe at a dead sprint. Wolfie was out of there fast.

And that little minx! The one with the red riding hood. Wolfie drooled. He wiped it off with the back of his paw. Words can't describe the feelings Wolfie had for Little Red. He called her that, though he knew she was at least a decade his senior, which enticed him all the more. Grown enough, but Wolfie wasn't intending to spoil this experience with a premature provocation. He had time to enjoy Little Red a little longer, for temptation resisted only sharpens the sensation. Every good wolf knew this, and ours was one of the best. I do say was, as he's sadly no longer with us, in case you were wondering. It's been some time, so I'm comfortable talking about it now.

It was now or never for Grandma. Every day was a day too late to wait. Wolfie was determined to have his way. Time was ripe. Off to Grandma's he would go. But who do you think he ran into while following the path? Little Red Riding Hood, picking flowers, a basket of baked goods set down beside her just as dawn broke. Wolfie was less surprised than you'd think. He'd caught Little Red on this path before at about this time. He'd watched her heading into town in the late afternoons. And sometimes he saw her in the garden, or in the kitchen, or in the forest hereabouts at other times of day. Once he took a peek in the window while she slept. He'd seen Grandma more than that.

"Well, well, Little Miss Red! Fine to see you here. How do you do? Are you off somewhere, or can we lie by the river and let the blades of grass tickle our bare feet?"

"Wolf! I thought you weren't near. But here you are!" The honey in her voice drove Wolfie mad. Her hood hugged fetchingly around her. "It's been some time."

"The present is what matters, Miss." He was overcome at first and blurted out an salacious invitation unbecoming his role, but quickly composed himself for the occasion. Obliging, gentle and tame. "I'm glad to see you safe and well."

"Why thank you, Wolf! Thank the stars you're here! I'm all alone in the woods, and I was feeling quite afraid. Luckily the sun's come up just now. But I'd still appreciate an escort. I'd love to lie in the grass beside the river for a little. Will you accompany me? What a kind offer. Come with me over here." And she reached out for Wolfie's paw.

With his paw resting in her little hand, Wolfie was led a few steps off the path, but just for a moment. Wolfie knew this wasn't right. He savoured her touch, and one day it would be all the sweeter. "On second thought, Miss, you go on and indulge with a little nap near the river by yourself this time. I'm really not in circumstances which allow me to dawdle. Until we meet again, my dear." And Wolfie looked longingly over his shoulder as he turned from Little Red back onto the path he had chosen for himself. Wolf felt some of the pain of a loss, but it was overwhelmed by his sense of self-respect. All the sweeter he said to himself, and then grinned in anticipation. Even more so as he took off at a trot towards another fantasy adventure.

It would take a discerning observer indeed to make sense of Little Red at this moment. The slightest hint of disappointment, perhaps, well disguised? A vindictive, steely, self-determination that flashes by? A shrug and a shake of annoyance and acceptance. Then a shadow of concern. Was something not right about that encounter? Something about that Wolf. He didn't seems quite right. She had seen him, of course, just recently skulking about the cottage. Peeked in her window once, the cheeky prick. And his long looks at Grandma hadn't escaped her attention either. That son of a bitch wouldn't dare! Would he? Better be safe.

Little Red took off in a skip and a scamper through the thicket and thatch of the hairy undergrowth of the forest. Relieved in her belief that Wolfie would trot along at a measured pace, prognosticating his wicked plan, Red raced along the tops of the flowers with ease and grace, far outpacing Wolfie and arriving at the cottage with time enough to spare.

Grandma was informed of Red's flanking maneuver. A smile wriggled across her still handsome face, accompanied by a chirp of laughter. Then a rapid giggle and finally a guffaw. "Grandma, please hurry! Wolf will arrive any moment!" Grandma was persuaded to walk a village over and have tea with another member of the sisterhood, while Red performed a ritual punishment upon our presumptuous canine protagonist. Grandma's fire of inner pride was raging, stoked vigorously by Red's audacity. What a lady in Red she would be! One to shame the rest, herself included. And she pitied the wolf, to some degree. He would deserve what he got. But Grandma had often been thought the villain in her own stories, and could empathize with the Wolf. He was punished for his abhorrent proclivities, appetites of which he has little control. Grandma had often satisfied instinctual urges, even some deemed indecent by others, she had been branded for those proclivities by an enraged and increasingly nasty public. C'est la vie. The sisterhood understood. In the sisterhood she could confide. The trip would do her well. And off she went.

Red dashed from the cottage and clambered up the limbs of the cherished giant oak, just outside Grandma's fetchingly fenced yard. Lost among the limbs above the cottage, Sally spied Wolfie trotting impudently towards her, a dozen breaths off, straight up along the main path that might be used by the milkman, the miller, or the mayor himself.

Sally was not an evil creature. As of yet, Wolfie had been nothing but gracious and polite, providing one wasn't to comdemn Wolfie's perverted pubescent peeping behaviour. She would wait and watch as Wolfie chose to cross further and further beyond the morally dubious into the wilfully damned. But was it right to set bait? Thankfully not a puzzle we urgently must solve in the present predicament, thought Sally in her perch.

Wolfie did indeed skulk up to the side of the cottage, right through the yard, on light feet I will say to his credit. Wolfie wasn't some thumping mindless rock breaker. He was a noble creature. Yet as an apex predator, nothing was to stop him from committing breach of etiquette, or in fact law. The temptation was great, and perhaps none of us have the right to judge Wolfie. Perhaps he, too, might be regretful of his own weakness, a redeeming conciliation you might permit an rehabilitated addict. The fact remains, not having endured the same temptation, might we judge Wolfie fairly? Is it for us to say? An existential question for another time.

Wolfie popped up his front paws to the windowsill at Sally's side of the cottage, and they both had a good view, Wolfie of the interior of the empty abode, and Sally of Wolfie's length and girth. Sally saw as Wolfie's tail twitched and swished. Then all of a sudden Wolfie scampered thrice round the cottage, then thrice round himself right after his own tail in fit of frustration. "Damn mine eyes!" cursed a bulge eyed Wolfie. Exasperated, he made a mad dash right at the front door, and to the surprise of all concerned, burst straight through into Grandma's living room. You should be made aware, for the purposes of posterity, that not one dainty artifact littered about the cottage, on sidetables and sills, not a lamp or a curtain was damaged in any way. The solid oak swung wildly open on heavy iron hinges with a bang, but only the rug slid abrubtly before stopping. Even that felt under control, for Wolfie was indeed an admirable specimen of athlete, not anymore at the peak of his abilities, and yet still impressive and not to be underestimated. Wolfie never gets his due.

Now inside, what might he do? How would this work? Wolfie ruminated a moment. Another plan was evolving from the confused fog in Wolfie's brain. But it never got worked out. While Wolfie was taking a moment to compose his thoughts, he had wandered into the long fantasized bedroom. But his thoughts weren't on the moment. He wasn't enjoying anything as he wondered whether it might be best to bolt straight out that door and never come back. But he had sat down on the corner of the bed in the meantime, when he heard a bright, sing-song "Grandma! Are you there?" ring like a bell from just outside the cottage door. Something happened that never happens. And that's why we have this story. Wolfie panicked.

Wolfie scrambled under the generous down comforter, twice the size it need be, spread gloriously across Grandma's four poster oak frame ancestral magic bed. Each Red had said so to the next, for generations past. "This bed is magical!"

Wolfie cowered. It would have passed instantly. How silly of him? That delicious little red hooded delight? In a moment he could have pounced. But he was entranced by the little red butterfly flitting about the space as he shrunk under the cover.

"Grandma! I see you there under the cover. Your eyes are bulging, my dear, and moist! There, there, don't move. I'll straighten things right up. You just lay right there, Grandma." Sally distracted the Wolf by darting to first one spot, then another, arranging. Sally seemed to visit cabinets, and drawers, and desks, and closets, and all four posts of the bed, all the while Wolfie lay nearly motionless under the covers. "Here, Grandma, let me make you more comfortable."

Now, as to what happened next, I must say I'm as incredulous as the rest of you will be. Like it was the most natural motion in the world, as if Wolfie in the bed really were Grandma, Red lifted the covers and Wolfie with them into a seated position in the bed, with Red behind the mass of cover. "What long ears you have, Grandma!" And with deft contortion, Red slipped ropes prepared from the bed posts and knotted them, in one motion mind you, about both of Wolfie's forelimbs. This one act would foreshadow a glorious career of such maneuvers of expert dexterity for our Heroine, the bearer of a mantle, a long reverenced tradition in life, love, and literature.

Wolfie yelped and writhed ferociously, "What sharp teeth you have, Grandma!", but Red was undismayed and undistracted. Safe at the foot of the bed now, Red concentrated, and astoundingly lassoed one of the wolf's hindlimbs on her very first try. It was cinched to a third post in a thrice, and you bet the fourth followed faithfully. Wolfie was in her hands.

Do you see how fast it all happens? Once he's through the door, it's almost all over for Wolfie in a moral sense. He's in a bad way now. Might he deserve it karmically? Is that the question we're asking? Sure, Wolfie had a past of wolf-ing. He had a bitter fight to the death over this very patch of land he now claimed. And he'd eaten more than his fill. Even as a cub he callously let die his brother, for the sake of a buck that might have gotten away had he not given chase.

And what of intention, you might ask. And you would be right to do so. Wolfie certainly did harbour less than charitable intentions upon his arrival at Grandma's door. But he had done so on dozens of occasions previously as well. On all the others he had done no more than, admittedly all too frequently, trespassing upon a lawn. And are we to condemn intentions? How might we surmise accurately the intensity of those intentions. A passing whim or a manic obsession?

What has Wolfie done? But I know well you are waiting to hear what happens now. What's it all about. A knife is a little messy, but Red relishes the poetic moment. The Wolf tied up so prettily gave Red the time to consider. She made her way into the kitchen and rummaged in the medicine drawer for a scalpel she knew she'd find there, among sutures and such that Grandmas like hers were like to keep. She pulled the poker from the fire on her way back to the bedroom.

"Wolf!" and she gave him a good hard slap across the face, "I wish that would be enough for you to learn this lesson. But I know it's not. I'm going to hurt you and you deserve it. My family is umbillically attached to this land. On this land you must never pass. Grandma and I protect the wood at this outpost. We are born of your own spirit. And look at your here! I'm outraged, you nasty prick. We have looked upon you with a benevolent respect. But our relationship is always to be kept at a distance, lest we beckon you. Today I will scar you as a permanent reminder, and then may you go in peace, with a bit of you left here forever, a piece of you dead for what you have done."

Quick as a slip, that scalpel sliced off Wolfie's pride, leaving him sexless for the rest of his days. The iron poker cauterized a howling Wolfie, and he passed out in agony. Coming to sometime later, slathered in anti-bacterial ointment, expertly bandaged, just outside the fetching fence of the cottage, a very different wolf is born, bemoaning his wretched fate. Stopping to sob occasionally, when completely overcome, our poor wolf slunk gingerly away into the depths of the forest, never to be heard from again.

A saucy Sally pickled Wolf's pepper in an appropriate place, setting it on the shelf with satisfaction. Her inheritance of the red mantle was lighter now, light as a

feather, and Red skipped to at the rap on the
door.

"Well, Hello!" The axe slipped from
Will's hand, instantly under the spell of the
sisterhood. In a trance he allowed himself
led into the deceptively delicate living room
of the fetchingly fenced little cottage, just
on the outskirts of their town. And there we
must leave them, with respect for Little Miss
Red's right to personal privacy, a dignity
owed to all in the world of the Fairies.

The End

Acknowledgments

On any given tree a few of the branches are gnarled and twisted, warped and deformed, demented and how couldn't they be? Branches of our human kind will bear the oddest fruit. Some grow pleasant pigment, and to these we all salute. But some have moral defects, a malady that's most acute. Only few can tell the difference, only those the most astute.

Acknowledgment I owe to those that grew all gnarled before, suffered for their differences, invective on them poured. Some because they're ugly, some because they snore. Some because they're lazy and some because they whore. I'd let them all do as they like, the rules I do abhor. Freedom is my only rule, freedom I adore.

Tribute I will pay to these, the outcast, shunned, eschewed. The men and women not the same the world chose to exclude. Especially the ones that feel themselves by norms subdued. Without them fun would starve to death in a world of servitude.

Push back against the rules they make, don't let yourselves be jailed. Imprisoned, maybe not, yet still it's oppression thinly veiled, a moral tyranny forced on us, standards we've inhaled. Every law they pass on us is freedom but curtailed.

Author

I hate and I hate and I hate! But it passes in time. And what's left behind? I can't really say. It changes in seconds, it skews day to day. I am what I am at the moment, that's true. Be sure that I'm me when I'm talking to you. But look back in time, pick a day from the blue, what was it you said?, was that man really you?

That's me, your new friend, whose been tickling your ear. Hello, here I am, at the end of the book. A custom so odd, just peculiar and queer. You know me so well, but my hand lies unshook. And now here we are, not too late to appear. What's wrong, might I ask? Your look's so severe.

I get that a lot. It litters my path. My thoughts can incite in some others their wrath. Little Bo Peep just can't keep her legs shut, and Little Red Riding Hood works as a slut. Can't

I think so or say so if that's what I like? Would it be more PC if I wrote one a dyke? Lighten up, take it easy, your heat gives a tan. I'm not anything more or less than a man.

We're flawed, I'm aware. It's not really that bad. The littlest things make you crazy hot mad. I write for enjoyment, both others and me. I quite understand if it's the wrong cup of tea. I hope some will like it, the way that I write. I consider each story quite happy and bright. It brings me great joy to see them this way, strong, fearless, and willful, on a drunken moral sleigh, speeding recklessly downhill in a bout of cheerful play.

More to come, there is, for sure, in the stories after three. You've heard enough, for now, about the person that is me. What will I be tomorrow? We'll just have to wait and see.

Hell's Press

In prison does a man reside, he's earned it, and he knows. Admits, he does, the wrong he's done, the path himself he chose. Line up, he should, the days he's lived in neat and tidy rows. Recount, he will, all he has done in every one of those. Did he do what could be done? His lethargy oppose? The truth of what he is, he fears, the answers will disclose.